PRINCE
MARTIN

WINS HIS SWORD

BOOK ONE OF THE PRINCE MARTIN EPIC

BY BRANDON HALE

Illustrated by
JASON ZIMDARS

BOOKS IN THE PRINCE MARTIN EPIC SERIES:

PRINCE MARTIN WINS HIS SWORD

To Stefanie, who encouraged me, and Thomas, who let me tell him Prince Martin stories on the phone when I was far away from home.
—B.H.

To my children, who are my joy. And to all those who have encouraged me to make art.
—J.Z.

CONTENTS

CHAPTER 1

In a faraway land, many long ages past, a young boy awoke with his heart beating fast. As he opened his eyes, his dreams fled with the night—he'd had dreams of adventure and dragons to fight. And he'd dreamt of a dog with a lopsided grin, who had stuck by his side both through thick and through thin.

Martin threw back his covers and up he arose. The boy thought to himself as he put on his clothes: *Oh, that last dream was best; why did it have to end? I was having such fun and I'd made a new friend!*

Now at this point, you might make a quick mental note: the boy lived in a castle with drawbridge and moat. But besides the adults, the boy lived there alone. There were no other kids. It was all he had known. And the boy could explore the entire place since... his father was King and the boy was the Prince!

After eating his breakfast, he headed down toward the old armory, where all the weapons were stored. The room also housed armor for soldiers and knights, which they wore for their safety in battles and fights. There were helmets and gauntlets and shields and steel shirts to protect their whole bodies from insults and hurts.

An assortment of weapons was hung in straight rows. These were used to attack and drive off the King's foes. There were bludgeons and axes and maces galore; many longbows and crossbows—all ready for war. There were halberds and lances and partisan spears that were forged to arouse every enemy's fears.

But what Martin liked best was admiring the hoard's most amazing collection of *all* types of swords. There were arming swords, backswords—and *longswords,* to boot (whose mere

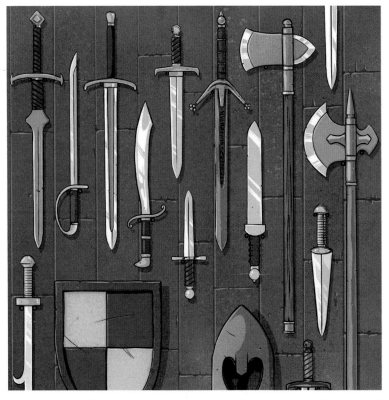

sight sometimes settled a violent dispute). There were claymores and tucks and the gladius, too— plus some broadswords and harpes (and a dagger or two). There were falchions and sabers for him to inspect. He could handle them all for he showed them respect.

But he longed for a sword he could have for his *own*—yet that was a thing the King wouldn't condone. He'd declare, "That is something that *someday* you'll get. But it won't be today for you're *not* ready yet. You must first prove your character. *Show* you possess the three virtues you've heard me repeatedly stress. Once you've proven you're brave, also loyal and true, then I'll give you a sword—one I've saved just for *you*.

"It's a marvelous short sword that's perfectly sized for a boy just your age; it's a blade to be prized. I know *someday* you'll win it, of that much I'm sure, but it won't be until those three virtues mature. Until then, if you need to deliver a sting, you can use your wood staff or your long leather sling."

The boy thought of these words, which the King always said. He would not disobey; he'd been way too well bred. With a big wistful sigh and a smile on his face, the boy picked up each sword, put it back in its place. Though he knew he would win his own short sword one day, he was getting impatient and tired of delay. But he wouldn't despair and his hope wouldn't fade: he would prove those three traits of which *character's* made!

Yes, he'd prove he was brave, also loyal and true. But *how* would he do it?

He hadn't a clue!

CHAPTER 2

It was still early morning; the day wasn't old. There was plenty of time for some fun to unfold. He'd explore in the forest—that's just what he'd do! The mere thought was exciting.

But fears arose too.

For the forest was wild, a mysterious place. Now his heart pitter-pattered; it quickened its pace.

Before leaving the castle, he checked all his stuff (in case trouble approached or the going got rough): a wood staff and a sling (you have heard about those), a canteen of cool water, and warm woolen clothes.

Now the boy was all ready to ramble outside. With his pack on his shoulders, he quickened his stride. Soon behind him, the castle; ahead, were the fields and the farmers who gave the King part of their yields. For when raiders tried burning the fall harvest crop, the *King* came with knights and they forced them to stop.

Now a farmer was sowing his barley and rye, when the sight of the Prince caught the sharecropper's eye. And this farmer, so glad of his King's strong defense, humbly took off his cap and he greeted the Prince: "It's a beautiful day to be out and about! Can I give you directions or help with your route?"

"I am bound for the forest," he said with a grin, "and I know how to get there, though I've never been. For I feel if I visit the forest today, an adventure might come—so I'm heading that way!"

"That sounds grand," said the farmer, "but *please* be aware that a pack of *wild hogs* has been lurking in there. Just a year ago past, they ran off from my farm. And now they've grown wicked and cause lots of harm. They are nasty and noisy, with bristly hair. And their sharp yellow tusks, oh, they slash and they tear! They destroy farmers' crops and they target the weak; and both pillage and plunder they constantly seek. If you see them approaching, you'd best climb a tree. Please do *not* try to run. There'll be *no* time to flee."

The boy thanked the kind farmer, who gave good advice. About that adventure, well, *now* he thought twice. But he thought of a phrase the King liked to repeat: "If you give into fear, all you'll know is defeat."

The young boy, he pressed on; he resolved to not quit.

And the farmer thought proudly: *Prince Martin's got grit*!

CHAPTER 3

At the edge of the forest, he stopped at a brook. The boy reached in the water and from it he took a few stones that all looked like they'd fly pretty straight: they were round, they were smooth, they were just the right weight. For the boy was quite skilled with a sling and a stone (he had practiced a lot— all those hours alone). The boy tucked them in tight with his sling and his gear. He'd be glad that he had them if hogs should appear!

Then on into the forest the young boy processed. And he felt the excitement well up in his chest. Ancient oaks, with great trunks, were two hundred feet tall. And their leaves were all golden that beautiful fall. The boy stayed on a path on which animals trod, and he'd hiked quite a ways when a crow loudly cawed!

The boy stopped and he froze; he was fully alert—because crows often caw if they're scared or they're hurt. There was trouble, he sensed, in the clearing ahead.

And then up rose the thoughts upon which fear is fed!

The boy shivered with fright from his head to his feet. He began to go home, beat a hasty retreat. But then *something* burst forth from the trees to his rear. The boy turned and beheld there a breathless brown deer!

The doe pled, "Help me, please! They've come after my fawn! They will not let us be. They refuse to move on. And the only thing keeping the villains at bay is a very brave stranger, who's barring the way!" The poor doe was exhausted; she looked pretty spent. Now he had a bad feeling he knew whom she meant.

"Who's come after your fawn?" the scared boy asked the doe.

"The four hogs!" she replied, "I assumed that

you'd know."

The boy felt his heart sink: it was just as he feared. Any courage he'd felt had by now disappeared.

Should he help or go home? The boy had to decide! And just how much help could a mere kid provide?

But he thought of the fawn, who'd been cruelly attacked—whose fate, he was sure, he *himself* could impact. Then the thoughts that had clouded his mind disappeared: he must do something now—do the thing that he feared!

The boy felt for his sling and he gripped his staff tight.

There was no time to lose—there were hogs he must fight!

To the doe, he declared, "I will follow your lead. Let us go help your fawn in his hour of need!"

CHAPTER 4

Toward the clearing ahead, the two turned and they sped. The boy hoped to himself that the fawn wasn't *dead*. At the clearing, they stopped at the edge of the trees.

Ah, but what the boy saw made him weak in the knees!

The four hogs had the fawn in a terrible scrape: they had cornered and trapped him—no chance of escape! There was growling and grunting and hair-raising yells. (Plus, the pigs were producing some punishing smells!) The four hogs had closed in on the fawn inch by inch. They had thought that the kidnapping would be a cinch.

But there stood in between the small fawn and each hog: a daring, determined, and dust-covered *dog*!

He was badly outnumbered.

The hogs were immense.

But the dog hadn't cared as he made his defense!

There had clearly been fighting and it had been fierce. The fur had been flying and hide had been pierced. You could tell that the coat of the dog had been white—but now it was marred with the blood from the fight. The dog's right ear was shredded; his left eye was scratched. And no one would say they were evenly matched.

Ah, but as for the hogs, you could tell with a look that the brave dog had given as much as he took! A few tusks had been broken and ears had been gnawed. If you'd seen the dog's courage, you would have been awed.

They were catching their breath in between brutal bouts. Hot steam rose from the hogs, from their backs and their snouts. And one sneered at the dog, "You are *not* gonna win. If you give us the fawn, you can save your own skin!"

The dog glared at him hard—looked him right in the eye.

"*Come and take him!*" he growled at the pig in reply.

CHAPTER 5

From the trees, the boy took this all in at a glance. Should he burst from his cover? For *this* was his chance!

He was stricken with terror. He wanted to run—or to climb up a tree till the fighting was done!

But he steadied his nerves; his composure, he kept. And though fearful, on into the clearing he stepped!

Martin yelled at the hogs as he made his approach! And the hogs were surprised— who would dare to encroach? (As he whirled a smooth stone in his sling overhead, Martin wished he was wielding a short sword instead!)

Martin thought he would miss with the first of his tries.

But he hit the lead hog between two beady eyes!

First a thump, then a thud: the thing dropped like a stone!

But *now* without doubt the boy's cover was blown!

Then two hogs left the fawn and they charged with a roar. But *now* he had courage he'd not felt before! He hit one with his staff; it was sure a hard smack. But the other hog knocked Martin flat on his back! There was blood where a tusk clipped him right on the cheek. And up close he could smell the hogs' foul musky reek.

As the hogs were regrouping, he got to his feet. Martin knew that in combat once more they would meet! He got back in his stance and he'd parry and thrust. Then he'd strike a hard blow for he knew that he must keep these villains off balance; they mustn't decide to *both* charge at once—or they'd have Martin's hide!

In the meantime, the dog had his hog one-

on-one. And the fiend that he fought weighed a full quarter ton. Oh, their fight, it was fierce like a terrible gale. For a while, it was hard to say which would prevail! The hog bit and he gouged and he kicked and he cussed, as the fighters produced a big billow of dust. But the dog had more heart. Also, *this* fight was fair. Of stealing the fawn, the pig soon felt despair. For his canine opponent was tougher than steel! And the coward gave up—he ran off with a squeal!

As the doe helped her fawn (who was safe but afraid), the dog limped to the lad (who now needed his aid). Then the dog and the boy fought the hogs side by side. They fought tooth for tooth and they fought hide for hide. And they fought well together; they fought as a team. Soon it dawned on young Martin: *It's just like my dream!*

And it dawned on the *hogs*, they were *not* going to win. They began to get scared. Their bravado wore thin. Then the bullies skedaddled; they fled from the fight. And they *never* returned, to the two deer's delight.

With the hogs soundly beaten, the coast was all clear: left in peace were the Prince and the dog and the deer. The boy couldn't believe it; had they really won?

He looked all around him: the deed had been done!

CHAPTER 6

With a whistle, he thought: *That was sure a close shave!* Then he turned to the dog, who had wounds that were grave.

The whole time he had suffered without a complaint. Ah, but now he passed out: the dog dropped in a faint. He'd been bitten and gored. He'd been battered and bruised. He'd been trampled by hooves, all roughed up and abused. His hurt eye had swelled shut and a leg wouldn't work.

Martin realized his duty, one he couldn't shirk.

So to lighten his load, he got rid of his pack. Then he groaned and he hoisted the dog on his back! He abandoned his staff and his long leather sling—the dog he now held was the critical thing.

Then the doe thanked the Prince with kind words so sincere, and the boy said goodbye to the two grateful deer.

Then he started his journey; his long walk commenced. But with each step he took, the Prince grimaced and winced. For the hogs hurt him too, hadn't let him off light: he had wounds of his own from that terrible fight.

The limp dog was real heavy—all muscle and bone. Oh, how the Prince wished he could walk on his own!

The Prince trudged a whole hour, and well did he learn how the dog's heavy weight made his poor shoulders burn. And he thought to himself: *When I reach that far crest, I must take a break. I must sit down and rest.*

So he stayed on the path to the top of the hill, where the fall air was cooler. He felt a sharp chill. From the heights, the Prince squinted and looked to the west. He had come a bit further than he might have guessed. And he saw, in the

distance, the castle's tall spire! Now his spirits rose up—but their plight was still dire.

The Prince eased the dog down to a dry patch of dirt. The dog slowly awoke but his body still hurt. The boy pulled out his water, gave some to the dog. Then he drank what was left. It had sure been a slog.

With a lopsided grin, the dog said he was glad to have fought by his side. And he said to the lad, "We sure gave those hogs heck; it was wonderful fun. I will never forget how those curs cut and run."

The dog's name was Sir Raymond (he went by "Sir Ray")—a brave errant knight from a land far away. Introducing himself with a shy little smile, Martin said he'd been wanting a friend for a while.

Then they looked to the west, saw the sun sinking low. Ray declared to the Prince, "Friend, it's time you should go. You can leave me right here; I believe I'm okay. When you make it back home, just send someone my way."

The Prince thought for a moment about

what he said. His *own* body hurt. And he longed for his bed.

Who would blame him for choosing to lighten his load?

If he left the dog lying, he *wouldn't* be slowed.

He could get home much faster—and *then* he could send a few horse-mounted servants to rescue his friend.

Then he thought about Ray, how he'd fought for the fawn. When he'd seen it in trouble, he *could* have passed on. He'd been badly outnumbered; it would have made sense. But instead Ray had rushed to the poor fawn's defense.

So Prince Martin decided that *he* wasn't taking the easy way out, though his body was aching. Martin made up his mind. The young Prince gave decree, saying, "Thank you, my friend... but you're coming with me!"

With a strain, the Prince lifted up Ray with a heft.

The boy took a deep breath.

And the two of them left.

CHAPTER 7

Thus, the Prince carried Ray; he continued his quest. As the shadows grew taller, he pressed and he pressed.

The sweat ran in his eyes, made it painful to see. There were times that he stumbled, went down on a knee. But he always arose, got back up and he marched—though he had weary legs and a throat that was parched.

With the sun sinking lower, he'd no time to rest—no matter how much his poor back would protest. He just plodded along and he bore the dog's weight, though his bodily aches didn't stop or abate.

And he saw, just before the sun set in the west, that the castle was closer. Hope rose in

his chest. Soon the Prince could perceive, by the high parapet: a most stately, familiar, beloved silhouette! He made out the King's crown and his shoulders' broad slope—he'd kept watch for his son, hadn't given up hope.

When the King saw Prince Martin, he shouted with joy, "Guards, raise the gate quickly, I've spotted my boy!"

The King flew to his son, who collapsed on the ground. And he scooped the pair up, both the boy and the hound. Then he headed back home with a powerful stride. Soon the king reached the castle and took them inside.

CHAPTER 8

For three nights and two days the young Prince slumbered on. And he dreamt of the dog and the doe and the fawn. The King sat there beside him, kept watch as he slept. He would not leave his son: faithful vigil he kept.

When he finally woke about dawn the third day, the first thing the boy did was to ask about Ray.

With a smile, the King said, "That brave dog will be fine. He did need a few stitches, but he didn't whine. And the royal physician did not disappoint: for he bandaged him up, got his leg back in joint. But Ray's eye can't be mended; it got a bad scratch. Although now he looks dashing—he's wearing a patch. And he's back on his feet now. He won't lie down and rest. He just asks about you—I can tell he's distressed.

"Martin, you got hurt too—quite a cut on your cheek! If folks mention your looks, that'll be their critique. But be proud of the scar and recall whence it came. From now on that brave badge will be linked to your name.

"Sir Ray said your adventure was more than you'd planned—but you rescued the fawn, drove the hogs from the land. He reports you fought bravely then stuck by his side. When the going got tough, upon *you* he relied. Son, you promised him help, then you stuck by your word—despite all the hardships and hurts you incurred. You refused to give up and you saw the thing through. Thus, you've proven you're brave, also loyal and true! Son, I'm proud of the way you conducted yourself," the King said, as he took a trunk down from the shelf. Then they both heard a sound—someone scratching the door.

The Prince *knew* who it was!

How his spirits did soar!

The King opened the door and Sir Ray bounded in! When he'd last been this happy, Ray couldn't say when! The dog leapt on the bed and he licked the lad's face. The Prince laughed and he gave him a mighty embrace! Ray declared, "I've been worried about you, my friend. I'm so glad that you're up, that you're back on the mend!"

Then the Prince and Sir Ray, they both turned to the King, who said, "Now you'll have *this* to deliver a sting." The Prince opened the trunk and he found there inside—a magnificent sword in a scabbard of hide!

If a moment ago he was achy and sore, with this sword in his hands, he was not anymore!

Its steel blade was exquisitely fashioned and wrought, and it bore fine engravings of famous fights fought. For the blacksmith who forged it had skill unsurpassed. Yet, the King could tell Martin had questions unasked.

"This was mine as a boy and my father's before. I took it with me when I first went to war.

And although it fits perfectly for a young boy, the sword's blade is quite sharp—and it *isn't* a toy. It belongs now to you, Son, to use in great need—never wield it in anger, revenge, or in greed.

"You have made me real proud: you've shown character, Son. And it *thrills* me to say that your sword has been won."

Now this first tale of Ray and Prince Martin is done, but the two friends' adventures had *only begun*!

THE END

FREE BONUS CHAPTER
Meet the mysterious forest-dwellers pursuing
the hogs—and discover the villains' fate!

Email the author at *brandon@princemartin.com*
to request the FREE bonus chapter.

ABOUT THE AUTHOR

When Brandon Hale was a young boy, he lived in South America. It was a great place to be a kid, and his mom let him play outside as much as he wanted. He had a dog named Okie, a slingshot, and an awesome tree house his dad built. The tree was full of pink mangoes, jabbering parrots, and fat iguanas! When he was older, his family moved home to Oklahoma, and he began second grade. His favorite classes were Reading and History. He still got to spend a lot of time outdoors, and sometimes his uncles would take him hunting—with their falcons! His favorite tales were *Treasure Island*, *The Swiss Family Robinson*, *Old Yeller*, and *The Hobbit*.

After finishing 19 years(!) of school, Brandon went to work as a lawyer. In 2001, a very beautiful lady agreed to marry Brandon. Now they have five great kids and live on the Oklahoma plains. Regarding Prince Martin, Brandon didn't even know he existed until he popped into his head one day! And when he had to go overseas for a long time in 2015, Brandon would tell his young son Prince Martin stories on the phone. In fact, the boy named some of the most important characters! Now Brandon wakes up real early every morning (when the house is unusually quiet) and writes about Prince Martin. *Prince Martin Wins His Sword* is his first book. Visit *www.princemartin.com* to learn more about the other books in the Prince Martin Epic!

ABOUT THE ILLUSTRATOR

Jason Zimdars is an artist and designer who has always loved to draw. He grew up immersed in stories of heroes and magic like *The Lord of the Rings*, *Star Wars*, *The Dark Crystal*, and *E.T.* He always came home from the movies or the library to draw all the amazing characters and places he saw in his imagination.

When his friend, Brandon, told him about Prince Martin he knew he had to draw him and all his friends, too. He can't wait to share more of Prince Martin's adventures with you!

Mr. Zimdars lives in Oklahoma with his family and dogs (who aren't nearly as brave as Sir Ray).

For More Information

www.princemartin.com
info@princemartin.com

Made in the USA
Middletown, DE
31 October 2021